In Plain Sight

RICHARD JACKSON

Illustrations by
JERRY PINKNEY

A NEAL PORTER BOOK
ROARING BROOK PRESS
NEW YORK

Sophie lives
with Mama and Daddy
and Grandpa,
who lives by the window.

He can see Sophie
come and go
call and wave goodbye,
hello . . .
as he looks out.

And after school each day, Sophie looks in.

"Here I am, Grandpa," she says.
"How was the morning?"

"Surprising," he says.
"I had me a paperclip, you know?
Nice and shiny.
Now it's vanished.
Help me find it, will you, with your bright
eyes?"

"Where?" says Sophie.

"That's just it, honey. You have to look."

If you lean close
you might hear Sophie say, "Oh."
And eventually,
you might hear her say, "There!"

"Good," says Grandpa. "Thanks, honey."

"Here I am," says Sophie on Tuesday.

"Ah, Sophie," he says,
"how was school?"

"Good . . . It was blue day."

"Well, I can see that."

"And how about you, Grandpa?
Today was—?"

"Regretful. Oh yes.
I had me a rubber band—
stretchy—boing—now . . .
boing, that band is gone.
Help me find it, huh?"

And eventually,
in plain sight . . .

"Here I am, Grandpa,"
says Sophie on Wednesday.
"Was today better?"

"Not so much," Grandpa says.
"Had me a drinking straw—
bendy, just right, you remember.
Now it's skedaddled."

"I'll look," says Sophie. "I wonder . . ."
And eventually, in plain sight . . .

"Good girl,"
Grandpa says.
"Thanks."

On Thursday, Sophie says, "Here I am,
Grandpa. Anything missing?"

"Well, wouldn't you know?
Grandma's favorite painting brush
for watercolors, child.
I'm missing that . . .
Can you help me, lovey?"

"I can try," says Sophie.
And eventually, in plain sight . . .

"Here I am, Grandpa.
Friday, at last."

"You bet, honey," he says,
turning his smile to her.
But wait . . . just look!

"Oh, Grandpa, you silly."

"Keep the dollar, Sophie.
Tomorrow," he says,
"you can buy yourself
something with it."

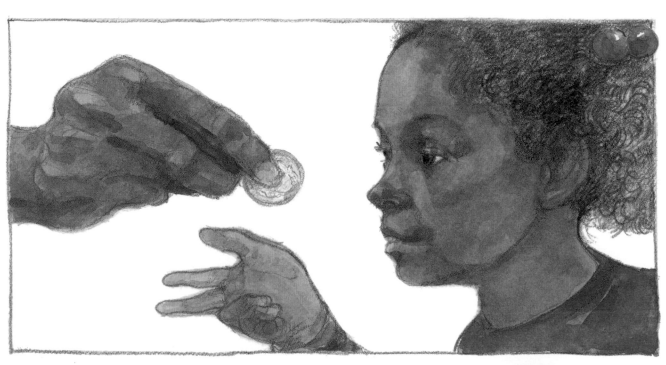

"Here I am, Grandpa," Sophie says. "Early today."

"No shopping? Well . . . best to save that dollar,
I guess. For college. Now, let's see . . .
Had me a . . . what?
A lemon drop!
Delicious to think of, but then
it just trotted off, unlicked."

"Don't tell me, Grandpa!"

And eventually, in plain sight . . .

"Good girl," says Grandpa.
"No, no, you have it."

Sunday morning, as usual.
At his door, Sophie starts to say,
"Grandpa, here I . . ."
but Mama hushes her.

"He's sleeping now."

Which gives Sophie an idea.
She whispers it to Mama.

Daddy laughs when he hears.
"All right," he says,
"if you tiptoe."

Here's Sophie, at her very quietest.
Her tiptoeing-est . . .
That curtain at Grandpa's window?
Well, keep your eye on it . . .

And eventually . . . where's Sophie?

Grandpa wakes. "Oh." Yawns. "Ah."

Behind the curtain, a commotion.
Wiggling,
            jiggling . . .
                        giggling.

"Sophie?" Grandpa says. "That you?
Why, I'll be!"

"Here I am!"
Sophie says.

"Like always."

l

For Brian Floca—

Seeker   Finder

—R.J.

For my great granddaughter Zion McKenzie Noel,
who helps me keep in touch with my inner child
—J.P.

Text copyright © 2016 by Richard Jackson

Illustrations copyright © 2016 by Jerry Pinkney

A Neal Porter Book

Published by Roaring Brook Press

Roaring Brook Press is a division of Holtzbrinck Publishing Holdings Limited Partnership

175 Fifth Avenue, New York, New York 10010

The art for this book was created using pencil, colored pencil, and watercolor.

mackids.com

Library of Congress Cataloging-in-Publication Data

Names: Jackson, Richard, 1935– author. | Pinkney, Jerry, illustrator.

Title: In plain sight : a game / Richard Jackson ; illustrated by Jerry
   Pinkney.

Description: First edition. | New York : Roaring Brook Press, 2016. | "A Neal
   Porter Book." | Summary: "An ailing grandfather and his helpful
   granddaughter play a unique game of seek and find"— Provided by publisher.

Identifiers: LCCN 2015034427 | ISBN 9781626722552 (hardback)

Subjects: | CYAC: Grandfathers—Fiction. | Games—Fiction. | African
   Americans—Fiction. | BISAC: JUVENILE FICTION / Family /
   Multigenerational. | JUVENILE FICTION / Family / General (see also
   headings under Social Issues). | JUVENILE FICTION / Social Issues /
   General (see also headings under Family).

Classification: LCC PZ7.1.J35 In 2016 | DDC [E]—dc23

LC record available at http://lccn.loc.gov/2015034427

Our books may be purchased in bulk for promotional, educational, or business use. Please
contact your local bookseller or the Macmillan Corporate and Premium Sales Department
at (800) 221-7945 ext.5442 or by e-mail at MacmillanSpecialMarkets@macmillan.com

First edition 2016

Book design by Jennifer Browne

Printed in China by Toppan Leefung Printing Ltd., Dongguan City, Guangdong Province

5   7   9   10   8   6   4